I0621901

Ten Thousand Years

By

Petar Kostadinov

Published by Petar Kostadinov

Through www.pajkpublishing.com

FIRST PRINTING

U.S.A

PAJKPUBLISHING

ISBN-13: 978-0615974576
(Custom)
ISBN-10: 0615974570

To My Father Vanco Kostadinov
Thanks for being there for me
I know you are an Eagle Now
With White Golden Wings
Peaceful and looking over us
Thank you for being there for me
When I needed you
You gave me life
And that life will be forever on
Till we meet up there in Heaven
And whatever planet you are on

Your Son and Author
Petar Kostadinov

CONTENTS

The First Chapter

I was about to imagine the new

dreams. The Future that was to come. The peace that would last on forever.

This Planet, is about to become new creation. In

the galaxy
for which
was sown
upon.
  How could
we distance
ourselves
from the past?
How can we
live on?
Without

knowing the right from wrong. But we must know that everything around us, was made for better.

These days we have been

longing for the Lord to come back to us. The sun to shine. For that rain that cried tears. Green everywhere.
  Remarkable, stronger.

Everything

that was abound
had been
promised to
fold and
become where
the success of
us, was to
cherish.
    I was talking

about forever. That time has come reality. That time came now. By the end of that road was a story. Story of words. Wisdom to share.

Many of us that stayed and protected the planets, were chosen to keep the life sacred.

It was promised to us that we could trust one another. For a

reason given.
Living in
sacred light was
that powerful
magic. We were
the hope that
brought us to
our endouvars
of life.
Where there is
light, there is

promise. And for those that placed us into darkness we have been given the chance to frolik to songs. To never give up. To begin what was new.

When The Day Came

When we
came to that
complete stop,
I realized that
we were not

home anymore. We were somewhere in the future of life.

Things were different here. Chairs, Cars, Trees, Places we bought our foods from,

Schools.

I have taken classes on this planet before. I was so incredibly curious. But back then, I was a child and as I grew older, I had to move at the age 21. Better place, better songs, as well better memory.

I was so lost as I have not been here in years. I am old as the sun. It

was possible
We are born.
Reality is, as
you age much
older you die.
No one knows
when there
time comes or
will be. Only
who is in
Heaven that

Protects it,
keeps it safe
and calls upon
the dear ones,
the chosen
Angels to
come join
him.
    He protects
us, without
doubt.

Many years
ago, we did
not know why
sickness occur.
We only tried
many cures.
Scientist were
developing the
way it should
be indent.
In hopes for

one day, we will have sickness free society. We would still have doctors. But those bad diseases that took away Innocent lives, such as my father's Liver, my family's friend; Uncle Kiro, who passed away from Cancer. And also my other family members such as my great-grandfat

her Todor,
who also got
that cancer;
including his
son.

It was
incredible. We
were on the
verge of
greatness. This
idea, and

reality that set in. I was amazed. I am just as futuristacly hopeful that for that moment of lifetime,

we were
proud to call
our selves,
miracles.

Moons That Never Frolicked

Certainly it was based on the river. The

one across the
mountains.
The one we
called Gods
own beauty,
clarity. The
where and
how. The
mystery of life
that when it
began, it was

just that.
"what is your
knowledge?"

'To learn'

"And where
do you want to
be?"
'Where ever
the road will

lead you on'
So, I set out to
ask him. To
find out why we
were to be set
out like this.
Why the rain
was falling so
sparkly. And
nobody is
getting hurt.

It felt on my heart. That line of beautiful songs playing. To be precise we had walked for miles now, and never had a thought of what was

about to
happen after,
came as close
and frivilant to
the eye.

This thing,
was some kind
of creature.
Nowhere in
the galaxy for

which we
never seen.
Where did it
come from?
Was it some
kind of
science project?
Was it the
sunsets of time
that forever
lost its

memory?
I could not
justified that.
But for the
signs that
brought back
the places it
was reaching
out to and
from.

*I knew
something but
nothing*

Here I was.
Sitting by the

end of the lake.
Perfect as it
was.
Somewhere in
the distance I
heard a heart
beating.
It had been
told years
before, that
every

remarkable
journey was
softer as the
rain falling.

The birds
kept on
chirping. What
was so
beautifully
crafted was

the sounds of
the rain
falling.
It could not
be so amazing
as it had been.
The
sustainable
future was
what was left
as the sea

parted from the skies.

When the song ended, we had to go back on our ship. We had to leave this planet. We had many places to visit and help in nature. To be precise. We were one step closer to the planet we were about to see. One and the only one that we must explore, for years to come.

I did not have
the courage at
this moment,
we needed
some sleep. I
was placed in
a position,
where every
time, someone
had called, I
had to just run

and help.
Flying was not
easy. Just as
though the
rain stopped
pouring, we
were there.
Stars,
unaccounted
by daily star
dust.

We left our families back on Earth for our job was much important, here in Space.

Where The Roses Bloomed

We
approached the
sunset moon.

The planet that never sleeps. The planet that peace forever exists.

Time in the past and future, nobody here owns anybody anything.

What Sets Us Apart

The difference between the man from Earth

and Mars, was
that inside of
our hearts we
knew to want
the same think.
We all want
peace and safety
for our
humanity. We
did have
however

different palms, skin, eyes are same.

Their skin is much yellowish according of the adjustment of the planets surface. The Heroic Gray Man, never became incredible mornings. I frowned upon this sizzle of life. As we landed there in 3098. I was given the captains permission to

explore and to
get back to him
what I saw and
who I met with.

Pretended that
I knew a lot. I
became the one
and only in
which after that
you know, they

gave me the hat to wear to observe and report back to the Ground Captain of Earth 1.

The ground seem fare. The way the robots we had send to

view and
explore back in
the early days
of the 21st
century.

The pictures
were taken,
people on the
internet raved
what we see and

what not was
there before.
But we did not
see was even a
slight
movement,
there had been
hidden clues
about it.

Every creature
took stone as

hideout and
they became as
the color of one.
So hidden such
intelligence.
   In the moment
we felt eager to
river the new
road, another
day chased the
moonlight. But

this robot never slept. Someone was always guarding it from NASA. Time was at the essence to rise for the new generations to find out if we ever been there before. If there had been something hopeful on the surface crawling. Yet, we knew there was water. Ice still exists. Never did disapate.

Curiosity knew where life might have been. So it marched and made a mathematical points. To be precise, it fined longed lines.

Studied it hard and achieved its mission.

When We Got There

For sure we knew where we ended up going.

What had mattered to us was the fact that we never knew the sunset ever have been reluctant in daybreak.

I looked for an answer. The question was

"How?"
 And then in the mere sense of time, it came to me. That everything here was the way it was left.
 Days have gone and come. Nights have just

begun. And the mere liking's of the peaceful praises that we were hearing it just proved to us uncredible. But yet, was it not? I just knew then and there and how and when. But did not ever know what for.

Predictability was given, we must regenerate and move on.

Beyond the Sun

When we left the 66th star from the second sun in the universe, we

discovered that
every moon and
every other
second star, just
beamed
heavenly. Life
was there. Water,
microbes living,
human beings;
somewhat like
us.

We stepped on the star and as we slowly got out from our ship on the boardwalk we saw buildings that looked like home. But what was it exactly? Was it mirage? I know it could not be. Home was far away. This humans were not the exact copies of us. God had other plans for them and each time we said hello, their hello

was different by
a briviation.
"Hello" He
glimpses at me
and says to us
'Why, hello.
We are here to
help you'
"Yes, we have
been expecting
you"

'Okay, what is your need?'

"Follow us please. I will show you. Precisely we have been born to create from a seed to a natural green foods to eat. Recently,

our has ceased
for some reason.
I know we don't
have much. But
we have to
show new
things come
alive"
    'But how did
you manage to
live so far with

this low food?'
  "We did save
some for times
like these. In a
space facility
across from the
library where
the people here
burrow and
share seeds
from each other.

It is set up in a great motion."

Notes

Notes

Notes

To Know
More About
The Author
Please visit

Amazon.com
Barnesandnobles.com
www.pajkpublishing.com